★ ★ HOTEL ★ ★
OF THE
GODS

BEWARE ᴛʜᴇ HELLHOUND

BY TOM EASTON

ORCHARD

HOTEL
OF THE
GODS

For Claire Wilson

ORCHARD BOOKS

First published in Great Britain in 2023 by Hodder & Stoughton

1 3 5 7 9 10 8 6 4 2

Text by Tom Easton © Hodder & Stoughton 2023
Cover and inside illustrations by Stephen Brown and Advocate Art Ltd
© Hodder & Stoughton 2023

A CIP catalogue record for this book is available from the British Library.

ISBN 978 1 40836 554 0

Printed in Great Britain

The paper and board used in this book are made from
wood from responsible sources.

Orchard Books
An imprint of Hachette Children's Group
Part of Hodder & Stoughton Limited
Carmelite House
50 Victoria Embankment
London EC4Y 0DZ

An Hachette UK Company
www.hachette.co.uk
www.hachettechildrens.co.uk

★ ★ CHAPTER ★ ★
ONE

Atlas Merryweather felt his backpack grow heavier and heavier as he trudged through the drizzle. He sighed and his glasses fogged up. It had been another bad day at school. And didn't it always seem that when you'd had a bad day at school the weather turned on you too, just to rub it in?

He stuck close to other people, hugging the shopfronts. *Hiding.* The last thing he wanted was for Eris Truckle, the class bully, to spot him and give him a second serving of the rough treatment she and her two friends had handed him at break. Eris lived near the shops on Thessaly Road. Atlas would have avoided the area altogether if it wasn't for the fact that his dad's fish and chip shop, **THE CODFATHER**, was there. Every Tuesday night he stopped by to pick up his tea. Even though Atlas loved fish and chips, he hated that it meant risking a run-in with Eris and her friends – who he secretly called the Furies after reading about these hideous creatures in one of his mum's books on Greek myths.

Atlas thought about gods and goddesses

a lot. His bedtime stories had always been about horned minotaurs and ice giants rather than fluffy bears and little pigs. Every night his mum would tell him a story, sometimes from a book, sometimes from her own memory. Sometimes the myths were Viking, sometimes Native American, sometimes from China or India. But the legends Atlas liked the best were the ones from Greece. Maybe it was because Mum's side of the family was Greek and came from Athens. Atlas had always felt a personal connection to the Greek gods and goddesses on Mount Olympus.

Atlas stopped around the corner from **THE**

CODFATHER, beside a low wall, and peeped to check the coast was clear. He could smell the delicious scent of hot chips and vinegar floating in the damp air. His tummy growled. But there was a good chance Eris and her chuckling Furies would be hanging around in front of the shop, insulting passers-by, squashing chips on the pavement and throwing mushy peas at cyclists.

Suddenly he was startled by something brushing against his ear. "*AAACH!*" he screeched, ruining the element of stealth. He spun to see a sleek black cat sitting on the wall, watching him. She had no collar, but that wasn't what drew his attention. It was the cat's eyes. They were a deep blue. Bright, clever and piercing.

"Hello, girl," Atlas said as his heart slowed its thumping. He reached out a hand and the cat leaned forward to allow him to scratch her ears. Atlas **LOVED** animals. All animals, but especially cats with piercing blue eyes. "You look hungry," he said, realising that the cat wasn't just sleek, she was thin.

Lifting his shoulders, Atlas took a deep breath and forced himself to walk around the corner and into the shop.

"**ATLAS**," his grinning dad roared from behind the counter. "I've kept you the **BEST** piece of fish." Atlas's dad was a large, jolly

man with a big, booming voice and a big,
bristling beard.

"You always say that," Atlas replied, rolling
his eyes but unable to avoid a grin. The smell
and warmth of the shop was comforting,
the damp customers gently steaming up

the windows as they stood waiting for their orders of cod and chips, or pie and chips, or sausages and chips, or chips and chips.

"But this time it's true! I spoke to the boat captain who caught it," his dad said, earnestly. "He told me it leapt out of the sea, right into his arms and said, 'Take me to shore at once! And there, let me be eaten by no one but Atlas Merryweather of Midham!'" Atlas's dad loved three things in life: stories, his family and food. He was a brilliant chef, his talent completely wasted in a fish and chip shop. He often told Atlas about the **AMAZING** restaurant he was going to open one day, and all the **FABULOUS** dishes he was going to cook.

"Why did the fish want me to eat it?" Atlas asked.

"Destiny!" Atlas's dad liked to talk about destiny, fate and universal harmony. He genuinely believed in all that new-age stuff. Atlas's dad handed him a warm paper-wrapped parcel. It smelled delicious. He also gave Atlas a milkshake.

"Is it . . . ?"

"One of my famous honey banana milkshakes?" Dad said with a wink. "Of course! Now off you run, boy of destiny."

Atlas smiled at him, then scuttled out the door. Still no sign of the bullies, thank

goodness. He turned the corner and was
surprised to see the cat was still there, as if
waiting for him. He stroked her head again,

but the cat seemed
more interested in the
contents of his parcel.

"You *are* hungry,"
Atlas said, tearing
open the package and
releasing a wonderful
smell of fried fish.

He broke a chunk of
soft white flesh off and held it out to the cat.
"CAREFUL, IT'S HOT!" Atlas warned, but
too late! The cat finished off the morsel in a

few bites. Atlas gave her a little more as the rain got heavier. "Sorry," he said. "I have to go. I'll give you some more if you're here next Tuesday." The cat looked up at him with those piercing eyes again, as if judging him.

Atlas scuttled off down the street. He didn't get very far before, through the gloom, he saw three figures blocking his path. He looked up, squinting through his rain-soaked glasses, and his heart sank.

"Hello, Atlas!" Eris said cheerily.

Atlas said nothing. There was nothing to say. You could ask politely, plead, shout angrily or cry. None of these ever had any effect on the Furies.

"Atlas," Eris said with a fake-friendly voice.
"Where is *Portugal*?"

"What?" Atlas asked, confused.

"Oh, never mind. But perhaps you could
tell me where *Peru* is, you know, on the map?
Or *Paraguay*?"

Atlas puzzled over this for a moment, then
sighed. "Oh," he said. "I get it. Because my

name is *Atlas*, right? Good joke."

Eris grinned and the other Furies shrieked with laughter.

"Look," Atlas said. "It's raining. Can you let me pass, please?"

"Is that a present for me?" Eris asked, ignoring his plea and pointing to his dinner. "How kind! It's not even my birthday."

"This is my dinner," Atlas replied.

Eris shook her head firmly and stepped forward, followed by her friends. "**NO**," she said. "It's mine."

Atlas thought for a moment. The sensible thing to do would be to hand over the fish and chips. But he was wet, cold and hungry.

He was also tired of being pushed around.

As the three big girls towered over him, Atlas squeezed the milkshake cup hard with his left hand. Thick, gloopy liquid SQUIRTED out of the straw, splattering Eris right in the face. She shrieked and fell back, wiping her eyes.

"I'M GOING TO GET YOU, ATLAS!" she screamed. But it was too late. Atlas was already halfway down the street, clutching his fish and chips triumphantly.

★ ★ CHAPTER ★ ★
TWO

When Atlas got back home to the flat on the 12th floor of Tower Block 7, Midham Estate, it was still raining and he wasn't grinning any more. He'd eaten his fish and chips on the way, as usual. His belly was full, but he was absolutely drenched and worried sick about what the Furies would do to him tomorrow. As he rummaged in his damp pockets for his keys, he felt something

brush against his leg. He looked down

through his foggy glasses to see the blue-eyed

cat looking up at him and

purring.

"You followed me?"

Atlas asked. "In the rain?

You silly cat. I've eaten the

fish and chips now!"

Atlas got the door open

and saw the cat rush in.

"**NO**," he cried. "**YOU**

CAN'T COME IN!" Pets

were strictly forbidden in his flat. He hurried

after her and found his sister, Ari, sprawled

on the sofa. As usual at this time, she was

watching **MEGA MASSIVE MANSIONS**, one of her favourite shows along with **PROPERLY PALATIAL PADS** and **HORRIFICALLY HUGE HOUSES**. The cat wandered around the little flat, exploring what it seemed to think would be its new home.

Ari watched the cat with a raised eyebrow.

"Bad move, Attie," she said. "Mrs McGrudy said she'd kick us out if you brought any more animals into the flat." Mrs McGrudy was their landlady. They were all terrified of her. She had bad teeth, bad hair and a bad attitude. She owned lots of flats in Midham and seemed to spend most of her time trying to evict people from them.

"She followed me home," Atlas said as he stood miserably, dripping rainwater on to the carpet. Thunder grumbled outside, like it was warning Atlas about something.

"Remember the mice you brought in last year?" Ari said. "And they escaped everywhere? Then there was the hamster you traded your console for. That had to go back the next day."

"I remember," Atlas said, glumly. The cat had sprung up on to the kitchen counter now and was sniffing at some dried-up Coco Pops from breakfast. The cat's tummy growled, nearly as loud as the thunder.

Ari was short for Ariadne, the name of a

princess from Greek mythology who helped Theseus out of the labyrinth. Atlas didn't think Ari had ever done anything like that. She'd once got lost in IKEA for three hours so mazes probably weren't her thing.

"Then you found that weasel and smuggled it into your room," Ari carried on, unhelpfully. "Though at least that took care of the mouse problem."

"Look, it's just until the rain stops, OK?" Atlas said, taking off his coat. "Mum and Dad won't be back for hours. I'll take her outside before they get home from work."

Ten minutes later, the cat was sitting on the desk in his room, watching him with her

unnerving blue eyes as he played his guitar.
Atlas was getting quite good. It was a shame
about his singing voice, though. He sounded
like a half-strangled pig being dragged
across a cattle grid. He imagined himself
in his fantasy rock band, *AFTERLIFE*,
playing his favourite song, *Rock God*, on the
Glastonbury Pyramid Stage. Maybe that
was his destiny! He hammered the strings –
SchWAAAANNNNGGGG!!! – and wailed
as the imaginary audience roared and crowd-
surfed and chanted his name. He was really
getting into this! Time for his signature guitar
move. Atlas stood, ran forward and dropped
to his knees, sliding across the threadbare rug

and playing
his favourite
power chord
to finish the
song.

SCHWAAAAANNNGGGG!

The crowd roared out his name.

"AT-**LAS**! AT-**LAS**! AT-**L**—"

"ATLAS!" shouted Ari, banging on
his bedroom door. "Keep it down or the
neighbours will complain to Mrs McGrudy!"

TWAANNGG!

"*OW!*" Atlas shrieked as one of the guitar strings snapped, snicking his finger. He sucked it and looked up at the cat, who was still watching him intently. At least the cat liked his music. That was a start.

"Maybe it wouldn't be such a bad thing if we were evicted," he told the cat. "I hate Mrs McGrudy, I hate this estate and I hate those stupid Furies."

The cat tipped her head to one side, listening.

"Also, the flat is kind of a dump," Atlas said as he fixed his guitar string. Mum and Dad didn't have a lot of money. They were always applying for jobs with better pay, but so far hadn't had much luck. "The windows are draughty. The walls are damp. The roof leaks and the boiler keeps breaking down. **MASSIVE ROCK STARS HEADLINING AT GLASTONBURY SHOULD NOT HAVE TO HAVE COLD SHOWERS!**"

Atlas had grown quite cross during this speech and shouted the last bit. As he finished, he was surprised to see the door swinging open and Mum standing there looking at him in alarm. She was home early and had heard everything he'd said.

Uh oh. He spun to look at the cat.

But the cat was gone. It had disappeared into thin air.

The next morning,

the family sat around the kitchen table eating

breakfast. This was the only meal they all ate

together and it was Atlas's favourite time of

the day. This morning, though, Atlas couldn't

concentrate on the buttery scrambled eggs,

Ari's new hairstyle or his father's crazy

stories. He was still thinking about the cat.

Where has she gone? He'd searched his room, then the whole flat. Had he dreamed the whole thing?

His thoughts were interrupted by a banging at the door. "I'll get it," he said, and went to the hall.

A young man stood outside. Atlas stared in surprise at his appearance. He had a strong, jutting jaw and dark hair. He wore a winged helmet and on his feet he had flashy trainers which were,

28

surprisingly, also winged. The man carried a satchel and, to finish off the outfit in a disappointing fashion, wore a dingy hi-vis jacket.

The man handed Atlas a scroll and said, "Gotta fly."

Atlas cried out in alarm as he saw the delivery man turn and *LAUNCH* himself over the railings into thin air. He rushed to the edge in time to see the man *FLY* off into the gloomy November morning, across the estate. Atlas saw there was gold lettering on the back of the man's jacket. It read HERMES.

Atlas took a deep breath, clutching the

scroll. *Am I going crazy?* he thought, his heart pounding. *First a disappearing cat. Now a flying courier?*

He walked back into the kitchen in a daze and handed the scroll to Mum. She raised an eyebrow but unfurled it and read. Dad wasn't paying much attention. He was telling Ari a story about a potato which had come to life yesterday at the fish shop and pleaded not to be turned into chips.

Atlas sat heavily, his mind spinning. What was happening?

"Oh," said Mum in surprise as she stared at the scroll. "*Ooooh!*"

"What is it?" Ari asked.

"Mum?" Atlas said.

"It's a job offer," Mum said. "Or rather, two job offers."

Dad watched his wife with interest.

"We've been offered jobs running a hotel," she explained.

"What?" Dad asked. "I didn't apply for a job at a hotel. At least not that I remember. Did you?"

"I don't know, we've applied for so many!" she said. "You're to be the chef. I am to be the general manager. They say they've been looking for ... for humans like us for a very long time."

"Humans?" Dad said.

"You are humans," Ari pointed out. "Sort of."

"Well yes, but . . ."

"The positions are live-in," Mum interrupted. "A big pay rise for both of us, and we'd be able to use the hotel's facilities when we're off duty." She dropped the scroll and grabbed her laptop, typing furiously.

"Does this mean I have to leave my friends?" Ari asked, frowning. "Because I'm really not sure if I want . . ."

But then Ari stopped talking, because Mum had turned the laptop around to show them the hotel's website.

"That is . . . **HORRIFICALLY HUGE**," Ari

said. "That is . . . **PROPERLY PALATIAL.**
That is . . ."

"**MEGA MASSIVE,**" Atlas finished, mouth
agape. The hotel was **AMAZING.** Hundreds
of huge rooms, a lobby with dozens of
chandeliers, a marble floor so shiny it was
basically a mirror, an infinity pool that
looked like it might actually stretch to
infinity, a spa, huge kitchens and a dining
room that would seat a thousand people.
The buildings were surrounded by rolling
green fields with glorious flowers, trees and
animals grazing in the distance.

"The spa . . ." Ari said.

"The kitchens . . ." Dad said.

"The animals . . ." Atlas said.

"The pyramid," Mum said.

"The what?" Atlas asked.

He peered closer. Mum was right; there was a **MASSIVE** pyramid in one of the pictures. Where exactly was this hotel? Egypt?

"You're going to accept the jobs, right?" Ari said, apparently having forgotten about her friends.

"**YES!**" Mum and Dad replied in unison. Then Dad rushed off to whip up some of his famous honey banana milkshakes to celebrate.

This is amazing, Atlas thought. It was as if

all their dreams had come true.

But as he took his first, glorious sip of milkshake, there was a feeling at the back of his mind. A feeling he couldn't quite shake.

A feeling that there was something really, really weird going on . . .

CHAPTER THREE

I t had been a REALLY long drive. Atlas had quickly lost track of the direction. But the satnav seemed to know where they were going. They'd started out through the city, then entered a forest, then crossed a long plain covered in mist and fog. Atlas had dropped off to sleep only to wake up halfway up a mountain.

Everyone had been very cheery at the start

of the trip, playing I Spy and word games and singing travelling songs. Mum had played all her Michael Bublé CDs, then started again from the beginning.

Now tempers had frayed a little. The car was quiet. They were all too tired to argue any more. Dad had stopped whistling. They hadn't seen any services for a hundred miles and even Mum had had enough of Michael Bublé. There was nothing to see out of the window because they were so high up they were immersed in a sea of cloud.

Atlas was about to ask if they were hopelessly lost when the satnav pinged and said, "Your destination is on your right."

The satnav's voice sounded even more relieved than Atlas. Maybe she didn't like Michael Bublé either.

Dad turned the car off the main road down a smooth driveway. The family saw two magnificent gateposts emerge out of the clouds. They were huge, thick columns with a stone sign above them to create an archway. The writing on the sign read:

Atlas frowned. *What does that even mean?*

"We're here," Mum said, excitedly. "We're actually here."

"OK, but where is here?" Atlas asked, looking at the mountaintops.

"Here is here, Atlas." Dad said, nodding sagely. "And here is where you will always find yourself."

"OK, thanks, Dad," Atlas said.

Half a mile further down the smooth paved driveway, the clouds cleared and the hotel finally came into view. It was huge. The photographs had not done it justice. Dad pulled up in front and Atlas got out, stretching his legs and clutching his guitar.

"Wow," he said, looking around in awe.

"Interesting mix of styles," Ari muttered. "I saw something like this on **COLOSSAL CALIFORNIAN CRIBS**. But this is way bigger. "

Atlas saw what she meant. The main complex was marble, finished in a mix of Greek and Roman styles, with columns and arches. Then, by the sandy shores of a lake, there were small huts, with roofs made out of palm leaves. A river ran between the buildings, into the lake. Stretching over the river was a bridge painted in rainbow colours. On the far side there was what looked like a great hall with a vaulted timber roof.

Beyond that, Atlas could see the pyramid they'd noticed on the website.

"Ah!!!" Dad said, taking in a great lungful of the sweet mountain air. He whirled around, arms outstretched. "Destiny has brought us to this place."

"Nope. Satnav," Ari said.

Dad ignored her. "This is a place where we can be free," he said. "Where we can be happy. Where we can be safe ... *AAAAGH!*"

Atlas spun to see what had caused his father to cry out. A huge square hammer was hurtling towards them out of the sky!

The hammer crackled with electricity and sizzled as it shot by them, narrowly missing

Dad and slamming into the ground. There was a **THUD** that made the earth shake and the hammer ploughed a furrow through the mud, scattering the family and ending up underneath the car.

"**SORRY!**" a deep voice boomed as a large ... no, huge ... no, **ENORMOUS** man bounded over from the direction of the wooden hall. He had long blond hair and the muscles on his arms were as thick as tree branches.

Atlas heard Ari gasp beside him.

"I was just practising my hurl," the blond man boomed at them. "You swing, then you hurl, you see. Very technical stuff. Didn't know there'd be mortals here."

"You mean here on the driveway in front of a hotel?" Mum asked, getting over her shock and suddenly cross at this man who'd nearly killed her entire family. "And what do you mean by *mortals*?"

"He was just practising his hurl, Mum," Ari hissed. "Leave him alone."

But the man was too busy retrieving his hammer to reply. With one hand he lifted the car and with the other he dragged the huge tool out from under it. Then he looked up at the staring family and grinned as he let the car drop back on to all four wheels with a CRUNCH.

"Let me help you with your chattels," the man boomed, scooping up all the suitcases at once with his free hand. He led the Merryweathers into the hotel lobby.

Now it was Mum's turn to gasp. The lobby was absolutely magnificent.

There were massive marble pillars, long shimmering curtains, wall fixtures glowing with a heavenly light and gleaming statues. The biggest statue was right in the middle and was of a muscular man with shaggy hair and a great beard. He held a lightning bolt over his head.

"Look," Atlas said, pointing. "It's Zeus!"

"**Where?**" the blond man said, dropping the suitcases in a panic. "Oh, you mean the statue. I thought for a second . . . never mind." He wandered off, brushing mud from his hammer, having apparently lost interest in the new arrivals.

". . . **YOU WERE WAVING AT HIM AT BREAKFAST!**" someone screeched. Atlas turned again to see two people descending the wide marble staircase. A very beautiful woman with long red hair was rushing down, while a handsome, muscular young man scurried along behind her, rending his tunic. "**DO YOU DENY IT?**" the man shouted tearfully after the woman.

She stopped and turned, raising a finger. "I do *NOT* deny it," she replied.

"**I KNEW IT**," the man said, collapsing theatrically on the steps above her.

"I *WAS* waving at him," she went on. "He was our *WAITER*. I only wanted to tell him my pomegranate was *TOO RIPE*. I have explained this *TWENTY TIMES*."

"**YOU TOLD ME YOU LOVED ONLY ME!**" the man cried tragically.

"Oh," Ari sighed, caught up in the drama.

Atlas sighed too. He hated lovey-dovey

stuff. This was just like the soap operas Mum watched, but with even worse acting.

The woman rushed back up the stairs and seized the man. "*I DO, MY DARLING. I LOVE ONLY YOU*," she cried. Then she kissed him passionately and slurpily.

"*Ewww*," Atlas said.

"*Ahhh*," Ari said.

Clutched in each other's arms, the couple rolled down the steps, still kissing. Bump, bump, bump, all the way to the bottom.

"*Owww*," Atlas said.

"*Ohhhh*," Ari said.

Mum cleared her throat, and finally the couple stopped kissing long enough to

notice them standing there.

The man got hastily to his feet, leaving the woman to dust off her green gown. He greeted the newcomers with a dazzling smile, his green eyes flashing. "Ah! You must be the new manager and cook!" he said, seizing Mum's hand and kissing it.

The woman in the green robe grew furious and tapped the handsome man on the shoulder. He turned and was greeted by a slap that rang around the lobby. The woman ran off, weeping.

"Oh bother," the man said. He rushed after her once more but this time it was him pleading for forgiveness.

"Well, they're exhausting," Ari said when they'd gone.

Mum let out a deep breath. "I think I need a cup of tea," she said.

"It does seem a very lively sort of place," Dad said.

"Don't mind them," a new voice said.

"They're always arguing." The voice belonged to a young man who Atlas thought looked like a surfer. He had long black hair in locs and tattoos in detailed patterns up and down his wiry arms. His dark eyes twinkled mischievously.

As if to illustrate the point, Atlas heard something smashing in the next room, followed by a heartrending scream.

"Are they OK?" Ari asked the surfer dude.

"Oh sure, they're cool," he replied, nodding. "They'll make up again in a few seconds." He paused for a moment, then added. "To be honest, I like it better when Venus and Mars are fighting."

"Hang on, Venus and Mars?" Atlas asked. "Like the planets?"

"No, dude," the surfer said. "Like the gods. I'm Māui, by the way."

"Māui, the trickster from the Pacific Islands," Mum said. "He brought fire to people." She walked off to help Dad, who had lost his phone in the confusion.

Atlas looked at the surfer dude. His brain seemed to want him to drag him towards a truth that was impossible.

"Er . . . Mr Māui," he began.

"Just Māui, dude," Māui replied.

"So Mars and Venus . . . they are . . ."

"Gods. I thought we'd already covered this."

"And you, yourself . . . are a god?"

"I'm just a hero, dude," Māui said, shrugging his shoulders. "But nobody's perfect."

"So are all the guests here gods or goddesses?"

"I just told you, man," Māui said. "I'm a hero, not a god. But they let me stay as long as I give them all free surfing lessons. Loki can hang ten no problem, but Zeus is a goose."

"Um, Māui," Ari spoke up. "The man who brought our bags in just now . . ."

"The one with the hammer?" Māui said, grinning. "Yeah, that's Thor."

"The . . . the Viking god of thunder?" Atlas asked, eyes wide. *Of course*, he thought.

The hammer, the hair, the muscles! It was all starting to make sense. If gods and goddesses existing in the real world could make sense. That meant the bickering couple were Venus and Mars, the ancient Roman gods of love and war.

"Mum?" Atlas called. "Dad? Could you come over here, please?"

Mum and Dad trotted over.

"Tell them what you just told me," Atlas said to Māui.

Māui shrugged. "**Hey there, old gnarled dudes.** This is a special hotel. It's for **GODS** and **GODDESSES**. Oh, and very select **HEROES** who shoot tubes and organise an awesome lū'au.

Hope you're cool with all that."

"I **LOVE** a lūʻau!" Dad said. "I have many recipes." He ran off to unpack his cookbooks.

"So this is a themed hotel?" Mum asked, looking fascinated. "A special experience where the guests all dress up as gods and goddesses? Like Disneyland with thunderbolts?"

Māui winked at her. "At this hotel, you believe what you want to believe."

Mum grinned and rushed off to inspect the front desk. Atlas and Ari looked at each other in astonishment.

"Maybe we didn't explain it properly," Atlas said.

Māui laughed. "Some mortals, particularly

the older ones, just don't get it," he said. "It's like their brains won't accept the truth. They'll make up any old fantasy to avoid facing reality. They'll come around to the idea eventually. Give them time."

"They're trying so hard not to believe," Atlas said, watching his father unloading more bags from the car.

"That's how things are now," Māui said, almost sounding sad. "But just because people don't believe in gods any more doesn't mean they no longer exist – they're immortal. They just don't have much godding to do any more now that people worship TikTokers and YouTubers and K-pop stars instead of them. So that's why they hang out here, on permanent vacation."

"Sort of like a retirement home for gods?" Atlas asked innocently.

Māui frowned and looked around anxiously. Then he leaned in close and whispered. "This is NOT a retirement home, little dude," he said. "And you'd better not let Zeus hear you say that." He considered for a second and added, "Not that Zeus can hear much these days. He is 12,000 years old, after all."

Ari seemed unconvinced. "Prove it," she demanded. "I've never even heard of a god called Māui."

"Hero," Māui corrected.

"Fine," Ari said, impatiently. "I've never heard of a hero named Māui. What have you ever done?"

Māui thought for a moment. Then he brightened, as if remembering. "I created New Zealand?" he said.

Atlas gasped, but Ari didn't look impressed.

"And I brought fire to humans," Māui added. He clicked his fingers and a bright ball of flame appeared in his palm with a deep *WHOOMPF* sound, like when Dad started the gas hobs at the chip shop.

Māui grinned at them, not noticing that the ball of fire had brushed the curtains

behind him. Flames
licked up rapidly. Ari
let out a strangled
cry and pointed.

"FIRE!" Atlas
cried.

"I know, right,"
Māui said, nodding and grinning and waving
the fireball in his hand.

"THERE'S A FIRE!" Ari shouted.

"Yeah, dude, FIRE!" Māui repeated. "All
because of me. Let's get some steak and
sausages and we can have a beach barbecue!"

PHHSSSSHHHH went the fire extinguisher
as Mum raced across the room and put the

curtains out. Māui whirled in surprise, his fireball disappearing in a puff of smoke.

"Nice work, Mum," Māui said, grinning. "Looks like we hired the right dudes."

As Mum inspected the curtains, trying to figure out how the fire started, Atlas noticed a movement from the corner of his eye. He turned to see a cat approaching. A very familiar cat.

"Oh sweet," Māui said. "This is Bastet. She's the totally cool Egyptian goddess of the home. And of cats. But don't grab her tail. She hates that."

Atlas felt his jaw drop. It was the cat from outside **THE CODFATHER**. He'd recognise those piercing blue eyes anywhere.

"Hello again, Atlas," Bastet said, winking. Suddenly, in a silky, flowing movement, the cat transformed into a beautiful human woman with a black bob and blue eyes lined with kohl.

She was wearing a white dress, like Atlas remembered from history lessons when they'd studied Ancient Egypt at school. He couldn't help but notice she'd kept her cat ears and tail.

"I am so sorry I was

sleeping when you arrived," Bastet said in a silky purr.

"Babes, you sleep more than Zeus," Māui said, "and he slept right through the year 2019."

Bastet ignored Māui.

"What's going on?" Atlas asked, glancing at his mum, who was still inspecting the curtains. "Why are we here?"

Bastet brushed an invisible speck of dust off her gown and smiled. "Your family were chosen to become our new caretakers after a long search for the perfect candidates," she said. "It is a very specific job and we needed to make sure we chose people destined for the role."

"Even me?" Atlas asked in a small voice. He swallowed nervously.

"Especially you," Bastet said.

"Really?" said Atlas, unconvinced.

"You, Atlas, were willing to help a goddess in need of shelter," Bastet went on. "And the delicious offering you provided me . . ." Her blue eyes got a rapturous look in them.

Atlas frowned for a minute. "You mean the fish and chips?"

"NECTAR OF THE GODS!" Bastet cried. "Now, let me show you to your rooms. Māui, please take the bags."

Māui shrugged and sloped off to help Dad carry the bags upstairs. Bastet didn't take anything. Cats weren't known for their helpfulness.

"What happened to the previous caretakers?" Mum asked as she followed.

Bastet stopped.

"**Oh man**," Māui muttered, looking down at his feet.

Bastet turned, her expression cold. "I'm afraid the previous staff members rather let us down," she said. "The food was poor, they overslept, the pool was neglected and they simply **REFUSED** to clean the Augean stables." She turned and walked up the final few steps to the first floor.

"Oh dear," Mum said, looking at Dad, who

frowned. The Merryweathers hurried along after Bastet.

"The final straw," Bastet continued at the top of the stairs, "was when they forgot to re-order enough of Dionysus's favourite wine. He feathered them."

"**FEATHERED?**" Atlas asked.

Bastet pointed out of a window towards the lake. A couple of ducks were splashing in the shallows.

"That's them there," she said, silkily.

"He turned them into ducks?" Ari asked, horrified.

"Don't worry, the gods are all pussycats, just like me," Bastet purred. She shrank back into cat form and rubbed herself against Atlas's legs. "I'm sure no one will turn your family into ducks."

Atlas felt slightly relieved.

Until Bastet added, "As long as you don't mess up, that is."

CHAPTER
FOUR

The next morning, Atlas headed into the dining room, yawning. Dad came rushing over, bouncing with excitement.

"Isn't this great, Atlas? Isn't it wonderful? The guests *LOVE* my pancakes."

"That's great, Dad!" Atlas said with a big smile. To be honest, he still had doubts about this place. **LOTS** of doubts. But Dad seemed really happy here.

Atlas stretched and rolled his shoulders. Despite the comfortable bed and the palatial suite they'd been given, Atlas hadn't slept well. He'd dreamed he was a duck being chased by an enormous cat while a huge blond man threw hammers at his head. Some dreams weren't hard to interpret.

He grinned though, as he saw the extravagant breakfast buffet Dad had set out. As well as the pancakes, there were piles of eggs, mountains of bacon and a selection of sausages. There was a bewildering variety of cereals, platters of fruit, bowls of yoghurt, jam, honey and thick slices of home-made bread for toasting. *Dad must have been up all night*, Atlas thought. Just as well if he was to keep all the gods and goddesses happy. Some of them had big appetites by the look of things. One hairy Viking god had ignored the pile of warm plates and was loading up food on his huge wooden shield instead.

Atlas grabbed a plate and headed for the eggs, but suddenly a huge hand clutched his shoulder and lifted him off his feet. He found himself face to face with a giant of a god wearing a feathered headdress.

"**DELICIOUS**," the god said, inspecting Atlas. "**I'LL HAVE YOUR HEART GRILLED OVER A BRAZIER.**"

"My h-heart?!" Atlas squealed.

"**INDEED**," the god boomed.
"**HAVE YOU NOT HEARD?
BREAKFAST IS THE MOST
IMPORTANT MEAL OF THE
DAY.**"

"Now, Quetzalcoatl," Venus called over.
"Atlas is the chef's son. He is NOT on the
menu."

Quetzalcoatl looked disappointed but
reluctantly dropped Atlas, who turned to
thank his saviour. She was seated at a nearby

table with Ari. They seemed to be getting on
very well.

"Is it too much to ask that someone offers
a human sacrifice to me?" Quetzalcoatl
grumbled. "I'm the Aztec god of the sun, the
wind and knowledge, for goodness' sake.

It's been over a thousand years and a chap gets rather peckish." The big god sat at a nearby table, still eyeing Atlas hungrily.

Taking a deep breath, Atlas turned back to the buffet just as Mars approached and helped himself to a bowl of something labelled Ambrosia.

"I need energy," he told Atlas. "I've got a tennis match with Thor today."

Atlas tried a taste. It was porridge with honey. He took his eggs over to the table where Ari and Venus sat chatting. Ari was showing the beautiful goddess something on her phone.

"This is Chloe Glow," Ari was saying as

Venus squinted at the screen with a frown. "She's great with hair, but for make-up tips I like to watch Zoe Smiles."

"If you want to look beautiful," Venus said, "you should come to my salon."

"You have a salon?" Ari asked.

"Of course," Venus replied. "I am the goddess of beauty, after all. And nails."

"Of course you are, my darling," Mars said smoothly as he sat beside his love. They seemed to be between fights right now, but Atlas suspected that wouldn't last long.

Ari flicked an admiring glance over at Thor at the far end of the dining room. He was practising tennis serves using his hammer.

Suddenly Thor lost his grip, and with a great

THROOM the mighty hammer shot across

the room. A hurricane of wind followed,

scattering people and furniture in its wake.

The hammer itself narrowly missed Atlas and

took the legs out from under the groaning

buffet table. There was an enormous crash,

and Atlas whirled to see the table flat on

the floor, food everywhere and the hammer resting on top of a platter of eggs. Though now it was more like a splatter of eggs.

"**SORRY!**" Thor yelled, waving his arm around. "Just trying to get warmed up."

Mars glared at him. "We're trying have a romantic breakfast over here," he said.

Thor glared back, little thunderclouds gathering around his head. "You know, maybe you and Venus should swap roles. **I think you'd be better as the god of LOVE, since that's the score you always get in TENNIS!**"

Mars got to his feet, looking furious. "**Oh yeah? Well maybe you should be the god of . . . of, I dunno, GETTING YOUR BOTTOM**

KICKED. Cos that's what's going to happen to you later."

"**Oh, great comeback,**" Thor said, rolling his eyes. "**Come on, let's get this started!**" The two gods stalked towards the French doors, glaring at each other. Atlas went over to see his mother.

"Do you need any help, Mum?" Atlas asked as she began to clear up the mess.

"No thanks," she said, smiling at him. "That's sweet of you. Why don't you go and watch the tennis match?"

"OK, if you're sure," he said uncertainly. He still had the feeling his parents hadn't completely accepted the fact that they were living in a hotel with real-life gods and goddesses. But Māui's words came back to him. *Give them time.*

Atlas headed out through the French doors to the garden, where the tennis court was. Thor and Mars were already there, warming up, still hurling insults at each other. Thor was using his hammer as a racket. Mars held a short, flat sword. Atlas sat on a marble bench and watched the game.

It was a fascinating contest. Mars zipped back and forth across the court, his shots fluid and sure, both forehand and backhand, left hand and right hand. He placed spin on the ball, fired aces down the line and performed sneaky little dabs just over the net.

"Thunder god? More like blunder god!" Mars cried after a particularly sly shot.

Thor, on the other hand, just stood still and hammered the ball back with a sound like a cannon shot, usually aiming directly at Mars, as if he was trying to kill his opponent rather than defeat him. Thor's long arms allowed him to cover most of the court and he hit with such force that Atlas couldn't even see the ball as it rocketed back towards Mars.

"Take that, god of warts!" Thor thundered as the ball rocketed down the line and pinged off the hilt of Mars's sword. It disappeared up into the clouds, leaving a trail of white smoke. When it landed on the grass several minutes later, Atlas picked it up and put it in his pocket.

Mars won a few points by carefully placing the ball where Thor couldn't reach it.

Thor won a few points by hitting Mars directly in the centre of his forehead and knocking him unconscious.

Eventually things came to a head when the two gods disputed a line call. The argument grew more and more furious until Mars brandished his sword and Thor swung his hammer. Atlas decided it was probably time to leave.

Around the corner from the tennis court Atlas came across a shimmering blue swimming pool. There were sun loungers on the wooden decking around it, and several diving boards on towers. One was so high it was lost in the clouds. The pool itself was so deep he couldn't see the bottom. It was a hot day and the water looked inviting even if slightly murky. He wondered if he was allowed to swim in it, or if it was just for the guests.

"Go ahead, little dude," came a voice from

one of the sun loungers, startling him. "You look like you could use a swim." It was Māui, lazing in the sun, wearing a pair of brightly coloured board shorts.

"Is it safe?" Atlas asked. "It looks kind of deep. And murky. Is that algae?"

"Don't worry," Māui replied. "The water's lovely. Very refreshing."

Atlas hesitated, but it was very hot now . . .

He peeled off his shirt, and after a moment he took a deep breath, closed his eyes tight and dived in. The water was perfect. Not too cold, not too warm. He let himself glide downwards into the pool's depths.

But when Atlas opened his eyes, he

realised he wasn't alone. In fact, he was face to face with another swimmer. A swimmer with scales, horns, a long, spiked tail and dozens and dozens of huge, great pointy teeth set into a jaw the size of a van.

It was a water dragon!

CHAPTER FIVE

Once a year, Atlas and his classmates had been taken to the Midham Leisure Centre and made to jump into the deep end of the swimming pool wearing their pyjamas. It was supposed to get them used to what would happen if they ever found themselves in deep water after, say, the boat they were on capsized, or their plane crash-landed in water, or they swam out too far in the sea.

Atlas had never understood why he might be wearing his pyjamas during any of these activities, but he went along with it anyway.

Unfortunately, none of these practice sessions had involved being attacked by a water dragon (while wearing pyjamas or not). So when this happened to him in real life, Atlas immediately panicked. He thrashed and kicked his way to the surface, then splashed and clawed at the water, screaming and swallowing a mouthful.

Choking, he started to sink again. His eyes widened as he saw the silvery beast thrash its long tail and come shooting for him through the greenish water, a murderous look in its bulbous yellow eyes.

This is it, Atlas thought. *I'm going to die.*

Just then, a strong hand clamped around his arm and he found himself being hauled out of the water. The dragon-thing came after him, its great head breaking the surface, its huge jaws slamming shut with a . . . CLICK!

. . . as they missed his ankle by a whisker.

The hand dumped him on the decking by the pool. Atlas coughed and spluttered as he lay in the warm sun, his heart pounding like a piston.

His rescuer turned out to be Māui, who was helpless with laughter. "I'm sorry, little dude," Māui said, wheezing. "I couldn't help myself."

Atlas stared at him with a look of betrayal.

"Don't . . . hee hee . . . don't look at me like that," Māui said, gradually getting himself under control. "I am . . . ha! . . . the trickster, after all? You can't trust me, oh no."

He clicked his fingers and a circle of flames sprang up around Atlas, who jumped in surprise, anticipating another attack, but then he realised Māui was just helping him dry off. There was another splash in the pool and the great head of the water dragon broke the surface, eyes flashing angrily.

"Let me introduce you, bro," Māui said. "This is Sìǎhai Lóngwáng, the Dragon King of the Four Seas. He's the Chinese weather and water god."

The Dragon King looked at Māui and . . .

ROARED. . .

"We don't get on too great," Māui admitted.

"Fire and water don't mix," Atlas muttered.

Māui nodded.

The Dragon King glared at Māui, then turned and slammed a great tail down into the pool, splashing them and dousing the flames.

"Hey," Māui cried, spluttering. "Not cool."

"You deserved that," Atlas said with a grin. He looked up at Māui and saw he was covered in slimy green algae from the pool.

"I guess I did," Māui agreed. He brushed off the slime.

"**GROSS**," said Atlas.

"We haven't had caretakers for a while," Māui said, looking sheepish. "Standards have slipped a little. But now you're here, everything's going to be cool, right?"

Atlas frowned. He wasn't at all sure he wanted to live in a place where water dragons tried to eat you and fire gods played mean tricks. Was that the role Bastet had chosen him for? Cleaning algae out of a pool? Some destiny.

"Now come on," Māui went on. "I'll give you the grand tour. You seen the stables yet? Speaking of slipping standards, you might want a peg for your nose. Hercules is supposed to clean them, but he always finds an excuse."

Māui led Atlas across a great lawn bordered with flowers. The stables were bigger than his school, and nearly as smelly.

Inside, Māui led Atlas to a large stall. Atlas gasped as he looked in.

"Is that . . . ?"

"Pegasus? Sure it is," Māui replied, leaning on a pillar. "Go ahead, he won't bite."

Atlas peered at him suspiciously.

"I'm serious, for once," Māui said. "Gods' honour."

Atlas stepped closer to the winged horse. Pegasus moved forward to meet him, nudging

his nose over the stable door. Atlas reached

out his hand . . .

. . . and Pegasus bit it.

"*YOUCH!*" Atlas screamed. He turned to

see that Māui had literally fallen over from laughing so much.

"I got you again," Māui said. "You should see your face."

But then something strange happened. Atlas felt Pegasus's soft nose brush against the back of his neck. He froze, expecting the animal to bite him again, but it didn't.

Māui looked surprised, and slightly disappointed. "Hmm," he said. "Maybe he likes you."

"Does he always bite people he likes?" Atlas asked sarcastically.

Māui shrugged. "He bites everyone. That's just his way of saying hello."

Atlas felt the magical creature exhale gently, its breath warm and sweet. He turned, and Pegasus nuzzled his shoulder. Gingerly, he stroked its silky mane.

"I've always wanted a pet," Atlas murmured. "I love animals. Especially magical ones you can ride."

"Pegasus isn't a pet," Māui said. "And if I were you, I wouldn't try riding him. The last guy who tried that was called Bellerophon and he got thrown to his death."

Looking into the creature's eyes, Atlas found it difficult to believe it could be dangerous despite the bite. It had really just been a nip, after all. Maybe this Bellerophon guy had just fallen. Riding a flying horse wouldn't be easy, after all. But maybe . . .

Too soon, Māui insisted that they go on. "I get bored easily, little dude," said the trickster. "And when I get bored, I tend to play tricks, if you know what I mean."

Atlas said goodbye to Pegasus and followed Māui across the lawn towards a low building made of wood and glass.

"This is the spa," Māui said as they went inside. The air was cool and relaxing harp music was playing. "This is where I get my locs done. They also do tattoos, manicures and pedicures, replace feathers and sharpen horns, if you've got them."

"I haven't," Atlas explained.

"Oh, and they do facials," Māui said. "Look."

Atlas turned to see Ari and Venus in reclining chairs, with cucumber slices over their eyes.

Māui winked at Atlas and put his index finger to his lips. Tiptoeing into the salon, he picked up a jar labelled **AVOCADO FACE MASK** and tipped its green contents into the sink. Then he scooped some of the swimming pool goo off his hair and put it in the jar. Whoever next got an avocado facial was in for a slimy surprise. Giggling, Atlas and Māui went back into the main hotel.

Urged on by Māui, Atlas went sliding down banisters and running down long corridors knocking on all the doors, causing bemused gods and goddesses to pop their heads out. Suddenly Atlas realised he was having fun. He'd almost forgotten about nearly being eaten in the swimming pool. As long as you kept an eye on Māui and his tricks, he was really fun to be around.

After a while, Māui led them into a grand ballroom. The room seemed to have suffered some damage recently. The curtains were burned, there were massive holes in the walls and part of the ceiling had collapsed.

"Were you attacked by ice giants?" Atlas asked.

Māui looked around at the destruction. "No, Mars and Venus had one of their little disagreements in here."

"They caused this damage during an argument?" Atlas asked in disbelief.

"It wasn't the argument that caused the damage," Māui said. "It was the making up afterwards. Come on, let's go."

"Tell me about Hawai'i," Atlas said as they carried on down the hall. "I've only seen pictures, but it looks amazing."

"It totally is, my dude," Māui said. "Forest and beaches, volcanoes and surf."

"So why are you here?" Atlas asked. "It sounds like Hawai'i is just one big holiday resort anyway."

"It is," Māui agreed. "But sometimes you just need a holiday from your holiday, am I right?"

"I suppose so," Atlas said, remembering the sign at the gate – HEAVEN AWAY FROM HEAVEN. His family didn't go on a lot of holidays. They'd never had much money. In a way, this new job was the closest thing to a holiday they'd had in ages. Maybe it wasn't so bad here. If he could just avoid being eaten.

Māui had stopped by a door marked

BASEMENT. There was a large sign on it which read:

DO *NOT* DISTURB
DO *NOT* ENTER
STAY OUT
WE REALLY MEAN IT
DO-NOT-GO-IN
THIS MEANS YOU
SERIOUSLY, YOU DO **NOT** WANT TO GO IN HERE . . .

"You should go down there," Māui said.

"What? Are you crazy?" Atlas replied. "Did you not read the sign?"

"Pfft. Signs," Māui said breezily. "You're not chicken, are you?"

Atlas was about to reply that he was chicken indeed. He was extremely chicken. He was hen out of ten. He was the biggest, cluckingest chicken on the free-range chicken farm. But then he stopped. He was having such a good time hanging with his new friend Māui. He didn't want it to end.

Māui might be a trickster, but he was a good guy. He wouldn't let Atlas do anything really dangerous, would he? Besides, Māui was a hero. He would save Atlas's bacon if

anything really bad was down there, just like
he had in the pool.

What was the worst that could happen?

Atlas took a deep breath and opened
the door.

CHAPTER
SIX

Atlas descended the steps slowly, heart thumping. This was scarier than facing the Furies at school. This was scarier than being sent to the head's office. This was scarier than Donald Trump's hair. The basement was dark and he felt heat blowing up towards him. What little light there was glittered off walls encrusted with veins of metal: gold, silver and bronze. And the music! Heavy metal. Loud.

REALLY LOUD. Thrashing guitars and booming bass and thundering drums with a high-pitched singer screeching over the top.

When he reached the bottom step, Atlas stopped to allow his eyes to adjust to the dim light. Who was playing this awful music? And why didn't they turn the lights on?

Atlas turned around, and in front of him was a tall red-eyed figure carrying a long two-pronged ... fork? The figure was pale-faced and wore a purple cloak over a band T-shirt that read *SCREAMING CORPSE – UNDERWORLD TOUR 1983*.

Oh no, Atlas thought as understanding dawned on him. *Hades!* It all made sense.

As well as being the god of the underworld, Hades was also the god of precious metals. So gold, silver, bronze ... and Screaming Corpse, the loudest heavy metal band in rock history.

"Um ... hello?" Atlas said, nervously backing away until he felt the rough wall behind him.

Hades threw the fork thing with perfect aim, pinning Atlas to the wall, one prong on either side of his neck. The god shouted something at him.

"What?" Atlas replied. "I can't hear you over the music."

"*DID YOU NOT READ THE SIGN?!*" Hades roared, stalking closer.

"I'm sorry," Atlas squealed. "I didn't
mean to disturb you, your highness. I just
... um ... heard the wonderful music and
thought I'd investigate."

Hades blinked at him, seeming surprised.
Then he stepped forward and yanked the

fork out of the wall. Bits of rock trickled on to Atlas's shoulders.

"*You like this music?*" Hades growled, cocking his head slightly. His breath smelled rank.

Atlas nodded. "I play the guitar myself, actually."

"*Heavy metal guitar?*" Hades asked.

"Umm, sure," Atlas said. At least, he knew the opening chords for Screaming Corpse's biggest hit – *Burn in Hell*. Everyone knew that.

"Well then, I suppose you're welcome," said Hades. "Sorry about the . . ." He trailed off, peering at the razor-sharp prongs of the fork thoughtfully. "I get so few visitors these days. Can't think why."

"Me neither," Atlas agreed, trying to breathe through his mouth to avoid the smell.

"What?" Hades asked.

"I SAID, ME NEITHER," Atlas shouted. "DO YOU THINK WE COULD TURN THIS MUSIC DOWN?"

"*Oh, of course*," Hades said. "*Alexa, turn down the volume!*"

"Alexa?" Atlas asked, surprised.

"Alexa is my demon servant," Hades replied. "She's very useful." Atlas blinked in surprise as a red demon darted out of a hole in the wall and turned the volume down on the stereo.

Hades waved at a chair. "Take a seat. What

did you say your name was again?"

"Atlas," said Atlas, glancing nervously at the stairs.

"Atlas?" Hades said. "Like the Titan who lost his cap."

"Um . . . what?" Atlas replied.

"Atlas . . . hatless? Get it?" said Hades, chuckling at his own joke.

"Oh, err, yes. Haha."

"You must forgive my little jokes. I am something of an amateur comedian. I once had a joke published in *Underworld Weekly* magazine."

"Congratulations," Atlas said politely.

Alexa brought them a pot of tea. "It's

been absolutely ages since I've had a good chinwag," Hades said. "And it's so good to find a fellow music-lover. Tell me, have you heard "*Kill Them All*" by *Total Annihilation*? There's a wonderful guitar solo and some very poignant lyrics once you interpret the guttural screeching."

"I haven't, no," Atlas replied.

"You really should give it a listen," Hades said. "What do you prefer, death metal or thrash metal?"

They had a long chat. Atlas was surprised to find Hades was easy to talk to, especially when he stopped going on about heavy metal bands. Hades told him a little about his life – he even got a bit choked up when telling Atlas how much he missed his beloved wife, Persephone, the goddess of spring. Alexa handed him a tissue and Hades blew his nose with a loud honk.

"Anyway," Hades said after he'd recovered. "That's enough about me. Tell me about yourself."

Atlas shrugged. "There's not much to say."

"Oh come, come," Hades said. "Tell me all about your life, your good deeds and your crimes."

"Crimes?" Atlas said, confused.

"How am I to judge your character," Hades went on patiently, "unless I know what you have done, both good and evil?" He smiled reasonably, showing a full set of long yellow teeth.

Atlas stared at him, his heart pounding.

"More tea? A biscuit, perhaps?" Hades asked suddenly.

"Err, yes. No," Atlas said, suddenly wondering if this was some kind of test.

"Nothing to say for yourself?" Hades asked, peering at Atlas in a way that suggested he could see right into the boy's soul.

"Well no, not really," Atlas replied. "I'm

just a kid, an ordinary, normal kid. I'm not particularly good . . . or bad."

Hades leaned forward, his long, thin nose stopping centimetres away from Atlas's face. "Do you have a coin?" the god asked.

Confused, Atlas dug around in his shorts. In one pocket he found the tennis ball he'd picked up earlier. He shoved a hand into the other one. Yes! A pound coin.

He handed it over to Hades, wondering where this was going.

"Since you can't, or won't, speak up for yourself," Hades said, his red eyes flashing, "we'll just have to leave this to fate."

"Leave what to fate?" Atlas asked him.

"Well, your destination, of course," Hades exclaimed, as if it were obvious. He flipped the coin and said, "*Heads, Elysian Fields; tails, Tartarus!*"

He caught the coin and slapped it on to the back of his wrist. He whipped his hand away and peered at the coin.

"Elysian Fields it is," Hades cried, standing and sweeping the tea tray aside with a clatter. "I'll take you there now! Alexa, clear this mess up."

"Actually," Atlas stammered. "I really

should be getting back upstairs. My mum will be expecting me. I should finish unpacking, and I need to practise my *Bloody Massacre* guitar solo ..."

But Hades was shaking his head. "Oh no," he said, his voice reverberating like an amplifier at a heavy metal concert. He reached forward and seized Atlas by his shoulder. "*It is time for you to put the mortal world behind you and to accept that you are dead.*" As he said this last word, it echoed in the basement room, bouncing off the walls and battering Atlas's ears. **DEAD** ... **DEAD** ... DEAD ... DEAD ...

"**DEAD?**" Atlas shrieked. "I'm not dead.

Why would you say that? I'm alive! Look!" He got up, wrenched himself away from the god's strong grip and took a step backwards. "Could a dead person do this?!" he said, doing some star jumps. Then he dropped and performed six quick press-ups.

"Come, come," Hades soothed, helping a panting Atlas to his feet. "It's not like I'm sending you to Tartarus to be tortured. I'm sending you to paradise!"

"I don't want to go to paradise," Atlas said. "I'm not dead. I just came down here for a dare!" He turned, hoping that Māui was coming down the stairs to explain it was all a big joke. But the trickster was nowhere to be seen.

"Look," Hades said in a reasonable voice. "Between you and me, I know you're not **REALLY** dead. But see it from my point of view – I've been alone down here for hundreds of years with nothing to do. I just need to claim a soul. One teeny, tiny little soul. That's all. No one will even notice you're gone."

"I will," Atlas whispered.

Hades's eyes flashed again. "*Alexa, LOUDER!*" he cried, and the music boomed out, hammering Atlas's ears. The god stepped forward, reaching out a bony hand.

Atlas screamed, turned and ran for his life.

He was fast, faster than Hades, but it was dark down there in the basement. Atlas soon got lost, stumbling over hidden rocks, banging into walls. The music screeched and thundered, disorienting him further.

In his panic, Atlas crashed into a flat, hard surface. He felt around in a panic and located a doorknob.

"*NOT THAT DOOR!*" Hades bellowed from somewhere behind him. But Atlas wasn't in the mood to listen to warnings. Whatever was on the other side of this door couldn't be worse than being chased by the god of the underworld, could it?

He gripped the doorknob and yanked the door open to be greeted by a blast of hot air, hotter than a furnace. He immediately realised that yes, there were indeed worse things than being chased by the god of the underworld, and they all seemed to be on the other side of the door he'd just opened.

A red glow lit the vast chamber beyond. Great firepits roared in the distance; a river of molten lava ran over a waterfall and away across the rocky floor. Screams, moans and wails filled the air. And there were **THINGS**. Horrible spiny, leathery things. Black and brown and red things with too many legs and great ragged wings.

"*YOU FOOL!*" Hades shouted as Atlas stood in horror looking at the terrible scene. "You've released them."

"Who?" Atlas replied, his spine dissolving into ice water.

"*THE MONSTERS OF HELL!!!*" Hades cried.

As they watched, the monsters turned to look at them. Eyes glowing, mouths champing, fur rising.

And then ... the monsters charged.

★ ★ CHAPTER ★ ★
SEVEN

A tlas and Hades fell back as the monsters hurtled out. Three hideously ugly winged women swooped down on Atlas, shrieking and plucking at his hair.

"*The FURIES!*" Hades wailed.

But the Furies were bowled aside by the next creature to emerge: a huge dog with three massive heads and slavering jaws. Atlas didn't need Hades to tell him who this was.

It was Cerberus, who guarded the gates of hell. The great hound barked wildly as it charged past, seemingly interested only in making its escape.

The third monster was a truly horrifying creature. It had the body of a lion, the head of a goat and the tail of a snake.

"*No! Not the Chimera!*" Hades shouted.

The beast breathed fire at Atlas as it ran past. He ducked just in time but felt the fiery blast singeing his hair.

There was a loud bang as the door slammed shut. Hades stood with his back against it, breathing heavily, his eyes wide. "This is bad," he said. "This is really, really bad. Worse than when Slaughtermatch split up."

"But you closed the door," Atlas said, clambering to his feet and patting his head to douse the smouldering hair. "Only a few monsters got out."

"*THEY ARE THE WORST ONES!*" Hades screeched. "*You don't know what you've done!*"

"It's your fault," Atlas replied hotly, annoyed at being blamed. "You were chasing me!"

"Those monsters had been safely contained for centuries," Hades hissed, ignoring him. "If you don't return them to the underworld, they will cause death and devastation in the mortal realm."

"You want ME to catch them?" Atlas asked, astonished. "Why don't you do it? You're the god."

"Alas, I can never rise to the surface," Hades said, shaking his head sadly. "I have been banished to the underworld and here I must stay. Besides, I have hay fever."

"Very convenient," Atlas said, shaking his head.

"You opened the door," Hades said with finality. "You must put things right." And with that, he swept off down the corridor, disappearing into the gloom.

Shaking his head at the unfairness of it all, Atlas found his way back to the staircase he had descended what seemed like a thousand years ago. He ran back upstairs to warn his family about the escaped monsters. Maybe he could convince them to bundle into the car and head back to Midham at top speed. Surely they could just let the gods deal with the problem?

But when Atlas emerged into the hotel lobby, blinking in the light, he was greeted by utter chaos.

The Furies were wreaking havoc as they swooped through the lobby, pulling people's hair. Atlas ran after them into the dining

room, where
they began throwing
plates of food around like
frisbees.

"*Psst, down here.*" Atlas
looked down to see his
mum and dad cowering under
the table. He slid under to join them, narrowly
avoiding being crowned with a soup tureen.
Mars was there too, peering nervously out
from under the tablecloth.

"I thought you were the god of war," Atlas
hissed at him. "Shouldn't you be fighting
them?"

"Those ladies are terrifying," Mars replied.

"Like three Venuses on a really bad day."

"I'm starting to wonder if you may have been right about the guests being . . . well, unusual," Mum said, peering out at the chaos.

"Finally!" Atlas said.

"They certainly don't seem very happy," Mum went on.

"Maybe it was the potato salad," Dad said. "I might have put too much vinegar in."

"Dad, it's not the potato salad," Atlas hissed. "They're the Furies from Greek mythology!"

"I can see they're furious," Dad said.

"Some people have strong feelings about vinegar."

"We need a plan," Atlas said. "I'm sure we can come up with something if we put our heads together."

"We could challenge them to a game of tennis?" Mars suggested. "Doubles?"

"There are three of them," Atlas pointed out.

"Triples?"

"Oh, Atlas," Mum said. "What have we done? I thought this was a chance for us to have a better life. We should never have brought you to such a dangerous place."

Atlas hated to see his mother looking so

sad and worried. He knew he had to put things right.

"Mum," Atlas said. "Tell me what you know about the Furies."

Mum gritted her teeth in concentration, then said. "The Furies are mythical beasts from hell. They tortured guilty people in the underworld. They are sometimes known as harpies—"

"But how do you stop them?" Atlas asked as a fruit platter smashed to the ground beside their table, spattering them with strawberry pulp. "Can they be captured?"

Mum considered his question. "Well," she said. "Back in the ancient times, people used

to leave libations – you know, sweet offerings –
in temples to appease them."

Sweet offerings? Atlas thought. Then a light
bulb went on in his head.

"Dad," Atlas said. "Do you have the recipe
for your honey banana milkshakes?"

"Recipe?" his father asked, aghast. "A master
chef does not need a recipe. To make food fit
for the gods, I need my heart to show me the
way."

Everyone nodded. Even Mars looked
impressed.

"And bananas, obviously," Dad added.

"Can your heart find its way to the blender?"
asked Atlas. "We've got libations to make."

Atlas darted out from under the table, followed by his parents. The Furies spotted them and began hurling cutlery at them. *Clink, clang, crash*. Atlas stumbled as he ducked to avoid a soup spoon and slid on a bunch of grapes, crashing to the floor. In a flash, one of the Furies landed on him, cackling madly.

Suddenly Ari was there, holding a shield. She smacked the Fury around the head with a great clang, sending her flying.

Atlas scrambled to his feet.

"Thanks!" he said to his sister. They raced into kitchen, Ari holding off the Furies with her shield (which was actually a silver tea tray).

"Get the milk, it's libation time!" Dad yelled, jamming a dozen bananas and an entire jar of honey into the blender. A huge crash was heard from the dining room and something thudded into the door with a splintering sound.

"**HURRY!**" Ari yelled as she and Mum held the doors shut.

Together, Atlas and Dad whipped up the mixture and poured it into three big glasses.

"This had better work," Atlas murmured as he picked up the tray of milkshakes.

Ari held the door open for him a crack and he slipped through. The dining room now looked like a war zone. The gods and goddesses who hadn't already fled were cowering behind upturned tables as the cackling Furies threw chairs at them.

"Ahem," Atlas said, trying to get their attention.

One of the Furies, carrying a chair leg, turned and glared. Then she tucked in her wings and dived . . .

STRAIGHT AT HIM!

Atlas held the tray with the milkshakes out in front of him, trembling. The Fury shrieked and knocked one of the milkshakes off the tray with the chair leg. She took a step forward. Atlas took a step back.

"Would you care for a—"

The Fury swung the chair leg again, knocking a second milkshake off the tray.

This wasn't going the way he'd planned. Atlas looked up at the hideously ugly creature in terror as she towered over him, grinning maniacally, the chair leg held high.

He thought about dropping the tray and running away. Then Atlas remembered another time when he'd been faced by a terrifying creature, outside Dad's shop. A different sort of Fury. Eris Truckle.

Atlas decided he wasn't going to run away.

He knew what to do.

He grabbed the last milkshake from the tray and hurled its contents right into the face of the advancing Fury.

Then just like that, she stopped.

He watched her long, black tongue dart out of her twisted mouth and lick the milkshake splattered on the side of her face.

Her eyes widened and she dropped the chair leg.

"*MMmmmm!*" she grunted happily.

The other two Furies came to investigate, and within seconds all three were on their hands and knees, slurping up the spilled drinks. Atlas gestured furiously at his dad, who was peering out through the kitchen door.

"More!" he said. "Make more milkshakes!"

Atlas was about to give a huge sigh of relief when he heard furious barking coming from the lobby. It sounded like three dogs were having a fight in there. But Atlas knew there was only one dog on the loose – Cerberus: the three-headed hellhound.

If the dining room looked like a bomb had hit it, the lobby looked like a group of bombmakers had had a really big bomb party in a bomb factory. The glittering chandeliers had been pulled down and sparkling glass pieces were scattered across the marble floor. Most of the windows were smashed and their curtains torn down. The reception desk was reduced to rubble and the banister had been torn free and swayed drunkenly. The stairs sagged alarmingly because a gigantic three-headed hellhound was sitting on them. Two of its heads were fighting over the golden statue of Zeus, chewing it like a toy.

The third head growled as it looked up at one of the few remaining chandeliers, where Atlas could see poor Bastet cowering in terror. The cat goddess clung to the cable, which was creaking alarmingly.

Atlas's heart flipped as he saw Cerberus preparing to leap.

Without thinking, he put his fingers in his mouth and whistled. Cerberus stopped and turned all three heads to look at Atlas.

Uh oh, he thought. *Maybe that wasn't such a good idea.* He sprinted off as the huge beast sprang down the stairs in pursuit, roaring in triplicate.

Racing down the long corridor back past the dining room, Atlas heard the thunderous padding of great hairy feet behind him, and hot, foul doggy breath on the back of his neck.

He ran faster.

Atlas dashed up a random flight of stairs, slowing the hellhound down as it squeezed up the narrow staircase. At the top, Atlas realised he was near his own room. He ducked inside and slammed the door.

He dived for the bed, hoping to hide under it, but the door burst open behind him with a great crash. The dog let out a bark, rattling the window frames.

Atlas felt the hair on the back of his neck stand up. He spun to face the beast in desperation.

One of the heads grabbed one of his new trainers and swallowed it whole.

A second head bit his pillow, sending feathers flying around the room like a blizzard.

The third head opened its great jaws and roared, showering him with stinky dog-slobber.

It's wrecked my room in about two seconds, Atlas thought. What kind of damage would the hellhound do if it escaped from the hotel, he wondered.

The dog leapt over the bed, forcing Atlas to dive out of the way. On the floor now, he pushed himself backwards, desperate to get away from the snapping jaws. One of the heads stretched out towards Atlas's guitar.

"**NO!**" he cried. He sprang up and slid forward, grabbing the neck of the guitar with his left hand. As he slid, the fingers on his right hand accidentally strummed the strings.

PLING!

The effect on the dog was extraordinary.

The beast stopped dead. All three heads cocked simultaneously, staring at him.

Atlas blinked in surprise. Had the music stopped the dog? Were his power chords really THAT powerful? He played the chord again. Louder!

SCHWRANGGGGG!

The dog whined and sat back on its haunches, watching him with six curious eyes. Its fur was no longer bristling. Its teeth were no longer bared.

Not taking his eyes from the beast, Atlas plucked a few strings, then launched into a slow ballad.

The dog settled down, listening intently.

He seemed to like the music!

Atlas started to sing, but one of the heads growled quietly and he stopped. *Fair enough*, he thought. *Just the guitar, then*.

Soon the hellhound's tail was wagging. As the song ended, Atlas cautiously reached out a hand and scratched one of the heads behind its ears. The other two heads craned towards him, demanding equal attention.

Atlas put some soft music on the radio to keep the atmosphere calm, and within a few minutes, Cerberus was lying on his back. The hellhound's hind leg kicked madly while Atlas rubbed his tummy. Atlas had seen some strange things in the last few days, but

this really took the biscuit. Three biscuits,
actually. One for each mouth.

But how was he going to get the dog
out of his room and back down into the
underworld? Then he remembered. The
tennis ball! He yanked it out of his pocket
and Cerberus was immediately on his feet.
His tail wagged eagerly and three tongues

flapped out of three grinning mouths.

Atlas threw the ball across the room and Cerberus went skittering after it, his paws slipping and sliding on the floor. After slamming into the far wall and a bit of squabbling between the heads, Cerberus retrieved the ball and brought it back to Atlas.

He was a genius! First, he'd charmed the Furies. Next, he'd tamed Cerberus. Everything was under control! *But wait...*

Atlas sniffed the air. *Is that ... smoke?* He heard a crunching sound coming from outside. Running to the window, he looked out and groaned.

He'd forgotten about the third monster.

The Chimera was by the pool, where it was busy eating the sun loungers.

"Hey!" Atlas called, rapping on the glass. "Stop that!"

The Chimera stopped chomping and

looked up, right at Atlas. It dropped the sun lounger.

Oh good, thought Atlas. At least this monster was being reasonable.

Then the Chimera opened its goat's mouth and breathed out a long and brilliant jet of flames.

Directly at him.

Atlas sprang back just in time! The blast of fire slammed into the window, shattering the glass and setting the curtains alight.

Heart pounding, he clutched his guitar and backed away as the blaze spread around the room. He looked around desperately for a fire alarm, or a fire extinguisher, or a bucket of sand even, but there was nothing!

"DOES NO ONE IN THIS HOTEL CARE ABOUT HEALTH AND SAFETY?" he screamed.

As smoke filled the room, he knew he had to warn the rest of the hotel's occupants. "Come on, boy!" he called to Cerberus. "We've got to get out of here."

Holding his hand over his mouth, Atlas ran out of the room and hurled the tennis ball down the corridor towards the main staircase. Cerberus went yelping and slobbering after it and Atlas followed. He didn't know how he was going to deal with the Chimera, but he did know he wanted to keep the massive hellhound between him and the fire-breathing monster while he figured it out.

"**FIRE!**" he called, banging on doors as he ran down the hall.

A door opened and a sleepy god in a hi-vis jacket poked his head out, presumably wanting to see what the noise was sbout.

"**HERMES!**" Atlas cried, overjoyed to see him. "You're the messenger, right? The messenger of the gods?"

"I guess," Hermes replied, rubbing his eyes. "At least I was, back when there was important stuff to tell them."

"Well, I have something extremely important to tell them. Right now," Atlas said, panting.

"Yeah, like what?" Hermes asked.

"Like there is an escaped Chimera by the pool and the hotel is on fire."

"OK," Hermes said, nodding slowly. "That does sound quite important."

"Umm," Atlas said. "Like, now?" Was he the only one who seemed to be aware of the urgency of the situation?

"Oh yeah, sure," Hermes said. And suddenly, like that, the messenger god was gone in a blur of hi-vis yellow.

By the time Atlas got downstairs, Hermes had done his work spreading the word. Gods and goddesses streamed out of the hotel, grumbling as usual.

"Since when did a bit of fire hurt anyone?" asked Māui.

"You're quite right," Thor agreed, holding his hammer. "Honestly, it's all such a fuss about nothing. But as I'm out here, I guess I'll practise my hurling . . ." He threw the hammer.

Atlas pushed past the hotel guests, trying to find his family.

To his relief, he spotted his sister. She was with three women with immaculate hair and make-up. Atlas peered at them, sure he recognised them from somewhere.

"It's the Furies," Ari hissed. "They've been at the salon. I don't know what was in the green goo we used for the facial, but it worked like magic!"

"Good work," Atlas said. "Where are Mum and Dad?"

"Here!" Mum said, emerging from the hotel holding a dustpan and brush. "Oh, Atlas!" she cried, throwing her arms around him. "Thank goodness you're safe."

Dad wheeled a cake trolley outside. Thor's hammer landed on it, squishing a plate of cupcakes and a platter of chocolate éclairs. Dad was too busy staring at the burning hotel to notice. "This is a nightmare! We've messed everything up. If we're not burned or eaten, then they'll probably turn us into ducks."

"Maybe not," Atlas said. "Mum, what do you know about Chimeras?"

"Well," she began. "According to legends, a Chimera has the body of a lion, with the head of a goat protruding from its back, and a tail that ends in a snake's head. Oh, and it breathes fire."

"Yeah, I know all that," Atlas interrupted, trying not to sound impatient. "I mean, how do you defeat one?"

"Oh gosh," Mum said. "Defeat one! They

are very powerful. But if I remember correctly, one was defeated by Bellerophon, who shot him with an arrow from the back of Pegasus."

Atlas's ears sprang up. *Pegasus?*

Mum's eyes widened in alarm as she saw the look on his face. "Atlas, no! You are not going to fight a Chimera. **I ABSOLUTELY FORBID IT!**"

"This is all my fault," Atlas said. "If I hadn't gone into the basement, the hotel wouldn't be on fire. I just need to find a bow and arrow . . ."

"Are you listening to me?" Mum said. "I will not let you fight a Chimera. You're just a boy. Let the gods deal with it."

"Actually, forget the bow and arrow," Atlas

said, spotting Thor's hammer on the cake trolley. "I have a better idea."

Three minutes later, Atlas arrived at the stables, pushing his dad's cake trolley.

He rushed over to Pegasus's stall. The winged horse came up to him again, and he fed him a cupcake from the trolley. Then he picked up Thor's hammer and wiped the cream off it.

Māui's warning rang in his ear as he clambered awkwardly on to Pegasus's back. "I wouldn't try flying on one of these. Bellerophon tried that, and it didn't end very well."

But Pegasus seemed to know exactly what to do. He sprang out of the stall and through the stable doors, then before Atlas could say "Thor's hammer", they were in the air!

Atlas felt the rush of wind and a yawning, gulping sensation in his stomach. HE WAS FLYING!

The Chimera, upon seeing them, sprang into the air itself, roaring in fury. The two magical creatures circled each other warily while the gods and goddesses pointed and shouted encouragement. Atlas looked down and could have sworn he saw Māui taking bets on who would win.

The Chimera spat out a fireball. Pegasus

dodged at the last second, narrowly avoiding it, and Atlas felt the intense heat singe the hairs on his arms. Pegasus kicked at the Chimera with his back legs, landing a blow. The crowd below oohed and aahed as the battle went on.

"Yes!" cheered Atlas as Pegasus beat his wings, knocking the Chimera away.

A dark shadow fell across the sun and Atlas looked up to see the Chimera's long, leathery tail whipping towards them.

"Don't worry!" cried Atlas. "I've got this!" Instinctively, he swung Thor's hammer and scored a hit.

WHAM!

The Chimera screamed in pain and whipped its tail away.

But the force of the swing had unseated Atlas and he found himself slipping from Pegasus's smooth back.

"**AAAARRGGGHHHH!**" Atlas screamed in terror as he plummeted to the ground. Luckily Thor caught him, laid him on the grass and plucked the hammer from his grip.

"Thanks. I've been looking for that."

Now the Chimera was furious. It let out more blasts of fire, setting the roof of the hotel alight. As the flames travelled up the walls, Atlas saw Māui in the crowd, counting some money. He climbed to his feet with difficulty.

"Māui," Atlas shouted, staggering over to his friend. "**I'VE FAILED.**"

"I know!" Māui said, grinning and brandishing a thick wad of notes.

Atlas frowned. "Wait. Did you bet against me?"

"Nothing personal, little dude," Māui said. "I did tell you not to ride Pegasus."

"It's a disaster," Atlas said. "I've messed everything up and now we'll be turned into ducks."

"It could be worse," Māui said.

"How could it be worse?"

Māui shrugged. "At least Zeus hasn't woken up."

The hotel was going up in flames. And with it, Atlas's family's dreams. "Why is it up to me to fight the monsters?" Atlas shouted, suddenly cross. "You're all gods, why don't you fight the Chimera? Why don't you put the fire out? Why don't you—"

Cerberus trotted up to Atlas and dropped the soggy tennis ball at his feet. Atlas picked it up and looked at it thoughtfully.

"Dude," Māui said with a grin. "Don't look so sad. This is the most fun we've had in a thousand years. I wasn't sure what your job around here was going to be at first. But now I realise. You're the entertainment manager. And I think you're doing a great job.

FIVE STARS!"

Atlas ignored him. He knew exactly what he had to do. He turned and threw the ball as hard and as far as he could. It sailed high over the heads of the gods and goddesses, who looked up to watch it go. The ball came down on the patio area around the pool, where it bounced once, twice and, with a *plop*, ended up in the water.

Then Atlas looked over at Cerberus.

"FETCH!" he commanded.

CHAPTER TEN

Cerberus let out a thunderous bark and bounded across the garden after the ball. He bowled into Māui, knocking him over. Atlas saw the wad of notes fly into the air. "My money!" Māui cried.

As the dog approached the pool, Atlas saw the Dragon King's head pop out of the water, his eyes growing large.

The Dragon King roared in fury as

Cerberus leapt.

As the great hound bombed into the water, an enormous tidal wave swamped the poolside. The Chimera yelped as the wave of water hit his paws. Cerberus grabbed the ball

SPLLLAAAASSSSHHHH!

and clambered out, his heavy coat dripping.

"No, **NO!**" Venus cried as she guessed what was going to happen next.

Cerberus **SHOOK** his coat.

Slimy water flew everywhere, stinging Atlas's eyes and dousing the hotel guests.

Hissing and spitting, the furious Chimera darted towards Cerberus and let out a long plume of fire, aiming directly at the dog.

"Oh **NO!**" Atlas cried. He had become quite attached to Cerberus – he hadn't meant for the poor dog to come to harm.

The fire shot towards Cerberus, whose six eyes widened in alarm. But just before it hit, the Dragon King whipped his huge tail around, sending a tsunami of water towards the fire-breathing beast. Water met fire with a huge blast of steam.

But the Dragon King wasn't finished yet. He held up a trident and roared. Instantly clouds formed, lightning flashed, thunder rumbled and it began to rain. Great, heavy drops hammered down on the lawn and on the individuals that cowered there, both mortal and immortal.

The Chimera hissed and steamed in the deluge. Its fire was, literally, put out.

"Atlas, look!" Ari cried, tapping him on the shoulder. Atlas turned to see that the rain was also putting out the fire in the hotel. He heaved a huge sigh of relief.

The three shrieking Furies rushed past Atlas, trying to protect their new hairdos from the rain. "My hair!" one of them shrieked.

"You need to go somewhere warm and dry," Ari shouted after them. "The basement, perhaps?"

The Chimera trotted after them, looking rather pathetic.

Only Cerberus seemed to like the rain. He ran around the garden, splashing in puddles.

"I gotta admit, my dude, you did good," Māui said, giving Atlas a high five. "Even though I lost all my money."

"Your bravery has won you a table in Valhalla," Thor said, clapping Atlas on the shoulder and knocking him over. "You'll have to be dead before you can go there, of course."

"Can I take a rain check on that?" Atlas asked.

One by one all the gods and goddesses came up to Atlas to thank him for his courage and quick thinking.

Maybe the gods weren't quite as ungrateful as he'd thought.

"**CALL HIM OFF!**" someone shrieked. Atlas spun around to see Bastet, in cat form, being chased across the lawn by a delighted Cerberus. Atlas stuck his fingers in his mouth and whistled. Cerberus skidded to a stop and came trotting over. Bastet streaked off across the grass and disappeared into the hotel.

"I suppose I need to take you back down into the basement too," Atlas said sadly. He'd grown quite attached to Cerberus. He'd always wanted a pet to play with. Sighing, he led the massive beast across the lawn and into the building. They descended the steps to the basement together.

"I didn't expect to see you again," came a dusty voice from the darkness below.

"Oh, hello, Hades," Atlas said, nervously.

To his surprise, Hades gave Cerberus a massive hug, burying his pale face in the dog's shaggy fur. "*I wuv oo, Cerbie*," he cooed. "*I weally, weally missed oo.*"

Cerbie? Atlas thought.

Then it came to him. Hades was lonely. He missed his wife. He never had any visitors. That's why he was always so gloomy. That's why he had been so keen to chat to Atlas earlier, and to capture his mortal soul.

"You know what?" Atlas said. "Maybe it's

time you came upstairs for a while."

Hades looked at him doubtfully.

"Some sunlight and company would be good for you," Atlas went on.

Hades shook his head, looking miserable. "They don't like me," he said. "No one understands me. I think it's because of my musical tastes. And maybe because I sometimes trap them in hell and have my demons torture them with pointy sticks. They hold it against me for some reason. But I'm just doing my job."

"Once they get to know the real Hades, of course they'll like you," Atlas said. "I like you."

"You do?"

"Of course," Atlas said. "I really enjoyed our chat about music. I like your jokes. And we both like dogs, and . . . err, tea."

"And torturing mortal souls!" Hades added, brightly.

"Umm . . . well, maybe not that so much. Look, why don't we go up together now?"

Hades's cheeks turned rosy and he beamed with pleasure. "I'd like that very much," he said, nodding.

"I suppose we need to lock Cerberus back into hell," Atlas said. "I'll really miss him. He's a good dog."

"The best," Hades said. Suddenly his face

changed. "Unless . . . ?"

"Unless what?" Atlas asked.

"Well, I could always do . . . this!" Hades clicked his fingers, and Atlas was astonished to see Cerberus begin to shrink. Down, down, down. Two of his heads disappeared and a few moments later, the hellhound had become a rather scruffy little dog, with one lolling tongue and a wagging tail.

"No one has tried to enter the gates of hell in thousands

of years," Hades said. "Why would they? It's horrible in there. So I probably don't need a guard dog. I think it's time Cerbie was allowed to live upstairs for a while. If you don't mind looking after him."

"Me?" Atlas said.

"Of course, you," Hades replied. "I have affairs down below I must deal with. Souls to torture, fires to stoke, band practice. I can't be upstairs all the time. So . . . would you like to look after my dog?"

"I'D LOVE THAT!" Atlas said, dropping to his knees and patting Cerbie's head. He was a lot cuter as a small one-headed dog. Cerbie gave Atlas's face a slobbery kiss.

"He seems to like you," Hades said with a grin. "Just remember to keep him and Bastet far apart."

CHAPTER ELEVEN

"**I** don't know about this," Venus said, frowning as she brushed soot out of Ari's hair. The gods were helping Atlas's mum and dad tidy up. The Dragon King's clouds had cleared and the sun shone on the hotel grounds.

"It's really not necessary," Mum kept telling them. "It's our job. We're very happy to do it."

Mars led Pegasus back to his stable. Thor had volunteered to do the heavy lifting, which seemed to involve him throwing all the broken furniture out of the hotel grounds.

Hades was sweeping the tennis court. "Of course, the Ancient Greeks never won at tennis," he said. "Because of the Roman Umpire." He laughed wheezily at his own joke.

"I'm just not sure Hades is going to fit in," Venus went on. "There's a reason we put him in the basement."

"Because he's the god of the underworld, with the power to capture mortal souls and imprison them in tortured agony for eternity?" Atlas asked.

"No, we're not worried about that," said Māui, who wasn't doing much to help with the clean-up. "It's just that he tells such awful jokes."

Atlas nodded. That was true. "But look at how happy he is!" he said.

Hades's skin was still pale, but his eyes were no longer red. He stood taller and straighter and flashed his yellow teeth in a smile. Mum and Dad were being very polite to him and were even laughing at his jokes.

"*Where can you buy a creature that's half-horse and half-human?*" Hades asked, unable to hold his giggles in.

"I don't know," Mum replied dutifully.

"*At a shopping centaur*," Hades said.

There was a rustle of feathers then and Atlas whirled round to see Quetzalcoatl looking him up and down.

"A pity," the Aztec god said grumpily.

"What's a pity?" Atlas asked.

"I'd rather hoped you might have caught on fire," the god answered. "**I DO LOVE BARBECUED BOY.**"

Quetzalcoatl wandered off, leaving Atlas staring after him, wide-eyed.

"Speaking of fire," Mum said, as though an Aztec god hadn't just suggested he would like to eat her one and only son in a torpedo roll with fried onions and ketchup. "I do hope they're not going to fire us. We were on a trial period. And there has been a bit of . . . well, excitement." She gestured at the half-demolished hotel.

"We LIKE excitement here at Hotel of the Gods," a smooth voice spoke up, making everyone jump. Bastet appeared, in cat form, and rubbed against Atlas's legs. "It's been rather dull lately, in fact, until you showed up. We had to make sure your family were up to the job."

"So this has been a test?" Atlas asked with a frown.

"One you passed with flying colours,"

Bastet purred, changing back into human form. "I chose well when I chose you."

"So does that mean we can stay?" Mum asked.

"Of course you can stay," Māui said.

"And you won't turn us into ducks?" Ari asked.

"No, no," Bastet said. "You're safe. For now."

"We would be honoured to seat you at our drinking table," Thor boomed as he crossed the lawn, hammer slung casually over his shoulder. Ari glowed.

"I could not bear it if you left," Mars said, seizing Mum's hand and kissing it, before nervously glancing around to make sure

Venus hadn't seen.

"What do you think, kids?" asked Dad.

Atlas considered it. Today he'd nearly been drowned, burnt, eaten and clobbered by a hammer. He'd fallen off Pegasus, got lost in hell and been chased by a three-headed devil dog who had eaten his new trainers.

He looked at his sister and she nodded.

"Of course we'll stay!" Atlas said with a grin. A great cheer went up from the gods and goddesses as the Merryweather family had a group hug.

Atlas looked up at Māui, who winked.

"Hey dude, sorry about all the trickery and hijinks," he said. "Can we still be friends?"

"No problem, bud," Atlas said. Māui held out a hand and Atlas shook it.

BzzZZT!

A joke buzzer! Māui collapsed with glee. Atlas glowered at him, then grinned. *Never trust a trickster*, he reminded himself.

"Well, I think we should throw a party to celebrate," Venus said as they went inside the hotel. "We'll invite everyone. Hermes, go and tell all the gods and goddesses, wherever they are, scattered across the heavens and earth."

"And the heroes," added Māui.

"Oh man," Hermes groaned. "I'm gonna need some new shoes."

"Come, Ari," Venus said, grabbing her by the hand and leading her towards the spa. "You'll need a new hairdo if you're going to dance with Thor."

Ari blushed, but she didn't resist.

Dad's eyes lit up. "I've got a great recipe for hamburger patties. Fit for the gods themselves!" He rushed off to the kitchens.

"Oh dear. We need to finish clearing up before we have a party," Mum said, looking around the lobby.

"Never mind about that," Mars said, snapping his fingers to magically restore the curtains and chandeliers. Then he repaired the staircase and put the gold statue of Zeus back on its pedestal. "There, it's as good as new," he said, giving the statue a polish.

"Let's get this party started!" whooped Māui, heading outside.

A moment later, a great fire pit magically appeared in the lawn. Smoke floated through the air for the second time that day.

"We need music," Thor said.

Hades appeared beside him. "I believe I can help." Hades pointed his trident and a stage appeared out of nowhere. Alexa and a band of demons appeared and started to tune their instruments. Hades grabbed a guitar, winked at Atlas and began to play.

Soon, all the gods and goddesses were dancing to the heavy metal music. Māui threw some serious shapes as he bopped along next to Atlas.

Then, from the stage, Hades pointed at Atlas.

"Me?" asked Atlas.

Hades nodded and held out his guitar.

Atlas climbed on to the stage and took the guitar from the god of the underworld. And as the sun went down, shining gold on the cloud tops in the distance, Atlas played *Rock God* as the gods and goddesses danced and cheered. This was better than Glastonbury. Better than Wembley Stadium. He wasn't just playing *Rock God*. He WAS a rock god.

"**GO FOR IT, ATLAS!**" Mum yelled.

"**IT'S YOUR DESTINY!**" Dad shouted.

"**DON'T SING!**" Ari screamed.

The song was coming up to a good bit – the power chord. Atlas took a run-up, then dropped to his knees and slid across the stage, hitting the strings with a loud ...

Barking joyfully, Cerbie jumped on top of him, knocking him off the stage. They rolled over and over across the lawn, dog, boy and guitar.

Atlas lay winded, looking up at the sky

as Cerbie licked his face. He laughed as he stroked his new pet and listened to the demon band rock out. He was so happy he'd come to live at Hotel of the Gods – where every day was epic!

THE END

Looking for somewhere to spend eternity in comfort?

You'll find *luxurious accommodation* and
a *wide range of leisure facilities* at

This is what our guests have to say:

Dog-friendly hotel with easy access
to the River Styx. Basement room
was a bit hot, though.
Hades (Greek god of the dead)

Great location but the weather
can be unpredictable.
Thor (Viking god of thunder)

Disgraceful! New management allows dogs.
Bastet (Egyptian goddess of cats)

Do not play tennis with Thor.
He cheats.
Mars (Roman god of war)

Totally chill place apart from
the dragon in the pool.
Māui (Polynesian hero)

Tasty food, but no human sacrifices
on the menu.
Quetzalcoatl (Aztec serpent god)

This hotel is almost as gorgeous as I am!
Venus (Roman goddess of beauty)

A NEW GUEST IS CHECKING INTO HOTEL OF THE GODS... AND THOR ISN'T VERY HAPPY ABOUT IT.

VIKINGS ON VACATION

COMING SOON